READING CHAMPION

The Snow Globe Adventure

by Caroline Walker and Sara Ugolotti

W

Chapter 1

Dad parked the van in front of a small house.

"Here we are," he said. "Our new home!"

Mia looked at the house, and the grey sky

above it. Everywhere looked cold.

Mia used to live in a different country. It was

a lot warmer there. But her dad had got

a new job so they had to move house.

The one thing Mia was really looking forward to

was snow. She had never seen snow before.

She hoped it would snow all winter in this

cold country.

Chapter 2

Every morning, when Mia woke up, she ran to the window.

"When will it snow?" Mia asked.

"It's not cold enough yet," Dad said. "Just rain today. We can stay inside and unpack."

living Room

Clothes

Kitchen

One of the boxes didn't have a label.

"What's in here?" said Mia.

"I don't think it's ours," Dad said. "Maybe
the people who lived here before left it
by mistake."

Mia lifted the dusty lid. Inside she could see toys
and a woolly hat and scarf.

"It looks like it belonged to a child," Mia said.

"Can I take the box to my bedroom and have
a look at everything?"

"Yes, good idea," said Dad.

Mia lifted everything out of the box. There was

a teddy bear, a book about bears and

a painting of snowy mountains. Mia tried on

the hat and scarf, which felt snuggly and warm.

Her favourite thing from the box was

a snow globe. Two bears were sledging down

a snowy slope. It looked so much fun!

Mia wished she could go somewhere like that.

"I'd love to try sledging!" she thought.

Mia closed her eyes and shook the snow globe.

Chapter 3

Suddenly Mia felt cold air on her face
and the wind in her hair.

She opened her eyes. She was on a sledge,
zooming down a snowy hillside. As she sped
along, Mia saw trees and fields covered with
snow. In the distance was a frozen lake and
gleaming snow-capped mountains.

The sledge stopped at the bottom of the hill.

Mia looked around. There were two bears!

"Welcome to our snow-world,"

said one of the bears. "I'm Ted".

"And I'm Barney," said the other. "We love

playing in the snow."

"Did you like sledging?" Ted asked.

"It's ... amazing!" said Mia.

"Let's all go sledging then," cried Barney.

When the sledge stopped, Mia reached down to

touch the snow.

"It's not like I thought it would be," she said.

"It feels soft and crunchy at the same time."

"It's great for making snowballs," said Ted.

He made one and threw it at Barney. Barney

threw one back at Ted. It looked great fun.

Mia grabbed a handful of snow, rolled it

in her hands and threw.

"Got you!" she laughed.

Chapter 4

They threw snowballs until Mia's hands got really cold. She rubbed them together and blew on them, but they wouldn't warm up.

"Let's go to the cabin where it's nice and warm," said Barney. "Do you like hot chocolate?"

Mia grinned. She loved it!

While Barney made hot chocolate, Ted explained that children sometimes came from Mia's world to visit them.

"We hope you are enjoying your visit," Ted said.

"But you can go home whenever you want to."

Mia looked out the window at the snowy world outside. She didn't want to go home yet.

"'I'm warm now," she said. "Can we go back outside?"

Outside, they built a snowman and two giant snow bears. Mia learnt how to make a snow angel.

Chapter 5

By now it was tea-time. Mia was beginning

to feel tired and hungry.

"I think I had better go home now," she said.

"Can I come back another day?"

"Come back any time!" said Ted.

"It would be lovely to see you again,"

added Barney.

"Thank you so much," Mia said. She gave Ted

and Barney a big bear hug.

Mia and the bears walked through
the snow to the top of the highest hill.

Then they climbed onto the sledge.

"Ready," said Ted.

"Steady," said Barney.

"Go!" shouted Mia.

They were off, faster and faster ...

26

Suddenly Mia was sitting in her bedroom.

The snow globe was in her hands. She blinked

and stared around her room. Everything was

spread across the floor, just as she had left it.

She looked carefully at the snow globe again.

Did one of the bears wave?

"Tea's ready," called Dad, from downstairs.

Carefully, Mia placed the snow globe back

into the box and ran to tell Dad all about it.

Things to think about

1. How does Mia feel about moving home?

2. What does Mia discover has been left behind?

3. How does Mia react when she finds the bears?

4. How do you think the bears behave towards Mia?

5. Can you think of any other stories in which someone is transported into another land? What do they learn from it?

Write it yourself

One of the themes in this story is about dealing with change. Now try to write your own story about a similar theme.

Plan your story before you begin to write it.
Start off with a story map:

- a beginning to introduce the characters and where your story is set (the setting);
- a problem which the main characters will need to fix in the story;
- an ending where the problems are resolved.

Get writing! Try to use interesting noun phrases to describe your story world and excite your reader.

Notes for parents and carers

Independent reading
This series is designed to provide an opportunity for your child to read independently, for pleasure and enjoyment. These notes are written for you to help your child make the most of this book.

About the book
Mia and her dad have moved home – and country! Mia is not used to the cold at all. While going through some old boxes she suddenly discovers something magical and is transported into the world of a snow globe ...

Before reading
Ask your child why they have selected this book. Look at the title and blurb together. What do they think it will be about? Do they think they will like it?

During reading
Encourage your child to read independently. If they get stuck on a word, remind them that they can sound it out in syllable chunks. They can also read on in the sentence and think about what would make sense.

After reading
Support comprehension and help your child think about the messages in the book that go beyond the story, using the questions on the page opposite.
Give your child a chance to respond to the story, asking:
- Did you enjoy the story and why?
- Who was your favourite character?
- What was your favourite part?
- What did you expect to happen at the end?

Franklin Watts
First published in Great Britain in 2020
by The Watts Publishing Group

Copyright © The Watts Publishing Group 2020
All rights reserved.

Series Editors: Jackie Hamley and Melanie Palmer
Series Advisors: Dr Sue Bodman and Glen Franklin
Series Designers: Cathryn Gilbert and Peter Scoulding

A CIP catalogue record for this book is
available from the British Library.

ISBN 978 1 4451 7253 8 (hbk)
ISBN 978 1 4451 7258 3 (pbk)
ISBN 978 1 4451 7262 0 (library ebook)
ISBN 978 1 4451 8087 8 (ebook)

Printed in China

Franklin Watts
An imprint of
Hachette Children's Group
Part of The Watts Publishing Group
Carmelite House
50 Victoria Embankment
London EC4Y 0DZ

An Hachette UK Company
www.hachette.co.uk

www.franklinwatts.co.uk